# Lucy Longwhiskers

## Daisy Meadows

ORCHARD

# Contents

# PART ONE

## The Adventure Begins

CHAPTER ONE

# A Golden Visitor

Lily Hart picked up a bucket of lettuce leaves and stepped into the garden.

"Breakfast time!" she called, walking over to a rabbit run and tipping in the leaves. Three adorable bunnies hopped over to eat their breakfast.

Lily spotted her best friend, Jess Forester, coming towards her. Jess lived on the other side of the lane.

"I can't wait to spend the summer holidays helping in the hospital!" said Jess, giving Lily a hug.

Lily's mum and dad had set up the Helping Paw Wildlife Hospital in a barn at the bottom of their garden. They helped to make poorly animals well again. Like Lily, Jess adored all animals!

The friends walked towards the wildlife hospital. They passed a fawn with one leg in a bandage.

"I helped Dad fix his leg yesterday," Lily explained.

Lily's mum was in the barn already. "Just the helpers I need!" she said with a smile. Lily and Jess grinned. They were ready for work!

The girls fed the fox cubs and topped up the water bottles in the hutches. They chatted to the squirrels, mice and hedgehogs as they worked.

Just as the girls finished their jobs, Lily saw something move in the end hutch ...

A beautiful cat was inside the hutch. She had golden fur and green eyes.

"Lily, this cat was here last year, with a sore paw!" said Jess.

The cat suddenly darted outside.

"Come on!" called Lily. "Let's catch that cat!"

CHAPTER TWO

# The Magical Tree

Lily and Jess ran outside. The
golden cat sprinted across the
lawn and began to cross the
stream at the end of the garden.
She looked back at the girls
and miaowed.

Lily smiled. "Let's follow her!"
she said.

The girls
quickly crossed
the stream. In the
meadow beyond was
an old, dead oak tree.
But as the cat ran
to the tree, something
amazing happened.
Leaves sprang
from every twig,
shimmering in the

sunshine. Birds swooped down to the branches, and butterflies danced all around.

"It's come back to life!" Lily said with a gasp.

The cat was pawing at some strange marks on the tree trunk.

Lily pointed.

"Look! There's writing carved into the trunk."

The cat pawed at the letters again. Then she rubbed first Lily's leg, then Jess's.

"I think she wants us to read it out loud!" cried Jess.

Both girls read out the words "Friendship Forest!" and a small door appeared in the trunk.

Lily opened the door, and the cat bounded inside. A shimmering light poured out of the tree. Jess and Lily squeezed through the door, their skin tingling. They were standing in the middle of a beautiful sunlit forest!

"This is impossible," Jess said. "How can all this fit inside a tree trunk?"

Lily was trembling with excitement. "There's only one explanation …"

Together, both girls cried, "Magic!"

As Lily looked around for the golden cat, something else caught her eye. Inside another hollowed-out tree trunk stood a tiny cottage!

As the girls gazed around them, they saw more little cottages. One had tiny tables and chairs outside it. A sign said *Toadstool Café*.

From inside the café came the sound of voices.

Lily gasped. "Who lives here?"

## CHAPTER THREE

# Friendship Forest

"Those are the animals of Friendship Forest!" said a voice.

The girls turned around and saw that the golden cat had reappeared. She was standing upright on her hind legs!

"You can talk," Jess said to the cat, amazed.

The cat
laughed.

"My name
is Goldie.
Welcome to
Friendship
Forest! All the
animals here can
talk, just like me."

The girls gazed around them.

Goldie called, "Come out
everyone!"

Door after door opened and
animals appeared. There were
hedgehogs, cats, mice and birds.

"None of the animals have seen people before," Goldie explained. "That's why they were hiding."

A friendly-looking stork flapped down from a tree.

"Captain Ace, at your service," he said.

Two rabbits came out of the Toadstool Café. "Hello!" said one of the rabbits. "We're Mr and Mrs Longwhiskers."

Running out behind them came a tiny rabbit with a purple ribbon around her neck.

"I'm Lucy Longwhiskers. I'm so excited to meet you!"

Goldie smiled at Lucy. "Would you like to help me show Lily and Jess around?"

They all set off through the beautiful forest together.

"Why did you bring us here, Goldie?" asked Lily.

"I need your help," Goldie replied. "Friendship Forest is in danger. Yesterday I saw a strange woman in the forest. She picked a flower and it turned to dust in her hand!"

Lily gasped. "Who was she?"

"I don't know," said Goldie.

"Don't worry," Jess said, "we're here to help!"

"Thank you," smiled Goldie. "Now, let's explore!"

# PART TWO

## Friendship Forest in Danger

CHAPTER FOUR

# Grizelda

The girls found themselves
standing in front of a cave with
a red door. Beside the cave was
a bush covered in huge flowers.

"This is the Blossom Briar,"
Goldie explained. "As long as
it blooms, all the flowers in the
forest will too."

Just then, Lily spotted an orb of yellow-green light floating above the Blossom Briar. "What's that?" she asked.

"I don't know," Goldie replied, "but it's making my fur stand on end!"

The light floated down. Lily picked up Lucy and the friends ran inside the cave.

Through the window, the girls could see the orb of light growing bigger, then …

*Cra-ack!* It exploded, revealing a tall, thin figure.

She had a pointed nose and long, green hair.

"It's the woman I saw in the forest!" Goldie whispered.

Jess gulped. "Goldie," she said, "I think that woman might be a witch!"

Goldie opened the door
and went over to the witch.
"Why are you here?" she asked
bravely.

The witch's eyes glittered
coldly. "I want this forest for
myself," she sneered. "I just
have to get rid of all the silly
animals first …"

Jess and Lily ran outside
and stood next to Goldie. "Go
away!" Jess said.

The witch cackled. "Do you
really think two little girls can
get the better of Grizelda?"

She laughed and Lily felt a cold wind whip around her.

"Friendship Forest will be mine," the witch snapped. "I'll destroy Blossom Briar and all the flowers in the forest will die. Then the animals will leave!"

At that moment, four hideous creatures crashed through the trees. They smelled like rotten cauliflowers!

Grizelda smiled. "Welcome, Boggits – my loyal servants. Tear down the Blossom Briar and this forest is all yours!" Then Grizelda vanished.

## CHAPTER FIVE

# Bunny-napped!

"I'm afraid this is my home,"
Goldie told the Boggits
politely. "I'm sure we can find
you somewhere else to live."

The first Boggit shook his
head. "This be Boggits' home
now. We make new home nice
and messy!"

"Ladies first, Pongo!" growled a girl Boggit. She jumped up at the Blossom Briar, ripping off one of the flowers.

"Nice work, Whiffy!" shouted Pongo. "Do more!"

"No!" shouted a tiny voice. Lucy bravely hopped out of the cave and up to the Boggits. "Leave the Blossom Briar alone!" she cried.

With a mean grin, Pongo scooped the rabbit up in his big paw and ran off!

"After him!" yelled Lily.

The girls and Goldie chased Pongo as he crashed through the forest. But the Boggit had got a head start, and he was soon far ahead of them.

"He could have taken Lucy anywhere," Jess cried, searching under a large bush.

Lily peered around a tree, but there was no sign of Pongo or the little rabbit.

Goldie looked thoughtful. "The Boggits can't go into your world, so Lucy is definitely somewhere in Friendship Forest," she said.

Lily sat on a patch of moss, trying to think. Beside her, star-shaped blooms nodded in the soft breeze. Suddenly, one of the white blooms turned grey and lifeless.

"Look!" Lily cried. "The flowers are dying because the Boggits are hurting the Blossom Briar."

Just then, Lily spotted a
scrap of purple material. "This
comes from Lucy's bow!"
she cried. "The ribbon must
be unravelling. The pieces of
ribbon will lead us to where
Lucy is!"

CHAPTER SIX

# Mr Cleverfeather

The girls and Goldie darted
through the forest, searching.
They managed to spot three
more pieces of ribbon! But no
matter how hard they looked,
they couldn't find another
piece. The ribbon trail
had ended.

Suddenly, a loud buzzing sound from above made them jump. Then the surface of a tree trunk began rippling! A staircase appeared, winding around the trunk and up into the branches.

"More magic!" Lily breathed.

"Maybe Lucy's up there," Jess suggested. "Let's find out!"

The three friends began to climb up the twisty trunk. At the top of the tree was a ramshackle treehouse. There was no sign of Lucy …

But there
was an owl!
He wore a striped
waistcoat and a
monocle fixed in
front of one eye.

"These are my
friends, Lily and
Jess," said Goldie.
"Girls, this is Mr
Cleverfeather.
I think
we've found
his secret
shed!"

The girls gazed around. There
were half-finished gadgets
everywhere. Mr Cleverfeather
showed them his latest
invention, a leaf blaster!

Goldie told Mr Cleverfeather
about Lucy, the Boggits and
the Blossom Briar.

"Have you seen Lucy

anywhere?" asked Lily.

"I'm afraid not," Mr Cleverfeather replied. "But you could try my telescope."

Lily looked through his wooden telescope. Suddenly, she spotted something at the top of a tall tree. "It's Lucy!" she cried. "And she's in a cage!"

"Help me!" Lucy called.

"We have to get her out of that tree," Lily said in despair. "But she's so high up, we'll never reach her!"

# PART THREE

## Lily and Jess
## to the Rescue

CHAPTER SEVEN

# Boggit Blaster

"You must use my secret path," Mr Cleverfeather said, showing them a wooden path that snaked through the treetops.

Goldie, Jess and Lily ran off along the walkway. Soon they saw Lucy huddled in a cage made from sticks and rope.

"We'll get you out, Lucy!"
Goldie called.

Lily examined the rope.
"We need something to loosen
these tight knots …"

Jess smiled. She took her
pencil out of her pocket and
worked the tip into a knot.

The knot fell apart and the girls undid the cage.

Lucy jumped out. "Thank you for rescuing me!" she cried, hopping around their feet.

Lily hugged Lucy and they hurried back to Mr Cleverfeather's tree.

"Now we have to save the Blossom Briar," said Goldie. "But how?"

Jess gave a cry of excitement. "I've got an idea! Mr Cleverfeather, can we borrow your leaf blaster?"

Hiding behind a bush next to Goldie's Grotto, the friends could see that the Boggits had torn lots of flowers from the Blossom Briar.

Goldie's eyes flashed with anger. "Go, Jess!"

Jess pressed the leaf blaster's lever. *SWOOOSH!* A gust of air blew, sending trampled petals into a rainbow-coloured whirlwind.

"Nasty flowers in fur!" shrieked one Boggit. "Get off!"

"Pooh! I smell like flowers!"

another roared. "Disgusting!
Boggits, run away!"

"What's happening?" Lucy
asked.

"The Boggits only like dirt
and nasty smells." Lily smiled.
"So if we smother them with
pretty flowers, they'll go away!"

Soon, the horrible creatures thundered off into the trees.

"Hooray!" yelled Jess and Lily.

Then Jess noticed a familiar orb of yellow-green light zipping through the trees towards them ...

Goldie's fur stood on end. "Grizelda!"

CHAPTER EIGHT

# Watch Out, Grizelda!

The orb of light faded to
reveal Grizelda. Her green
hair flicked and twisted.

"Don't think that you've
stopped me," she screeched.
"I'll find a way to defeat you
all, and take Friendship Forest
for myself!"

With a snap of her fingers,
Grizelda disappeared.

Jess and Lily smiled at Goldie.
"We'll help keep Friendship
Forest safe, Goldie," Jess said.

The cat slipped a paw into
each of their hands. "Thank
you," she said, smiling. "Now,
let's take Lucy home."

At the Toadstool Café, Lily and Jess told their friends about their adventures.

"Hooray for Goldie and the girls!" they chanted.

Mr Longwhiskers asked about the poor Blossom Briar.

"Its blossoms will eventually grow back," Goldie said.

After that it was time for a delicious celebration tea! There was blackberry juice and strawberry fizz, honey sandwiches and slices of iced seed cake with cherries on top.

Soon it was time for the girls to go home. Goldie led them to a beautiful golden tree. She touched a paw to the trunk and a door appeared.

Lily and Jess said goodbye to their new friend, and stepped into the golden light.

Then they were back in the meadow near home!

Jess checked her watch. "Wow!" she said. "Time stopped while we were in Friendship Forest!"

The girls agreed to keep their adventures a secret, and walked back to the wildlife hospital.

"Having a good morning?" Lily's mum asked.

Lily and Jess smiled at each other. They said together, "It's been magical!"

The End

# Magic
## Animal Friends

Continue your reading journey
with the Magic Animal Friends
chapter books!

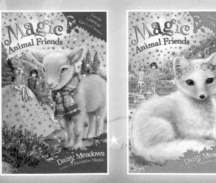

www.magicanimalfriends.com